families of a feather

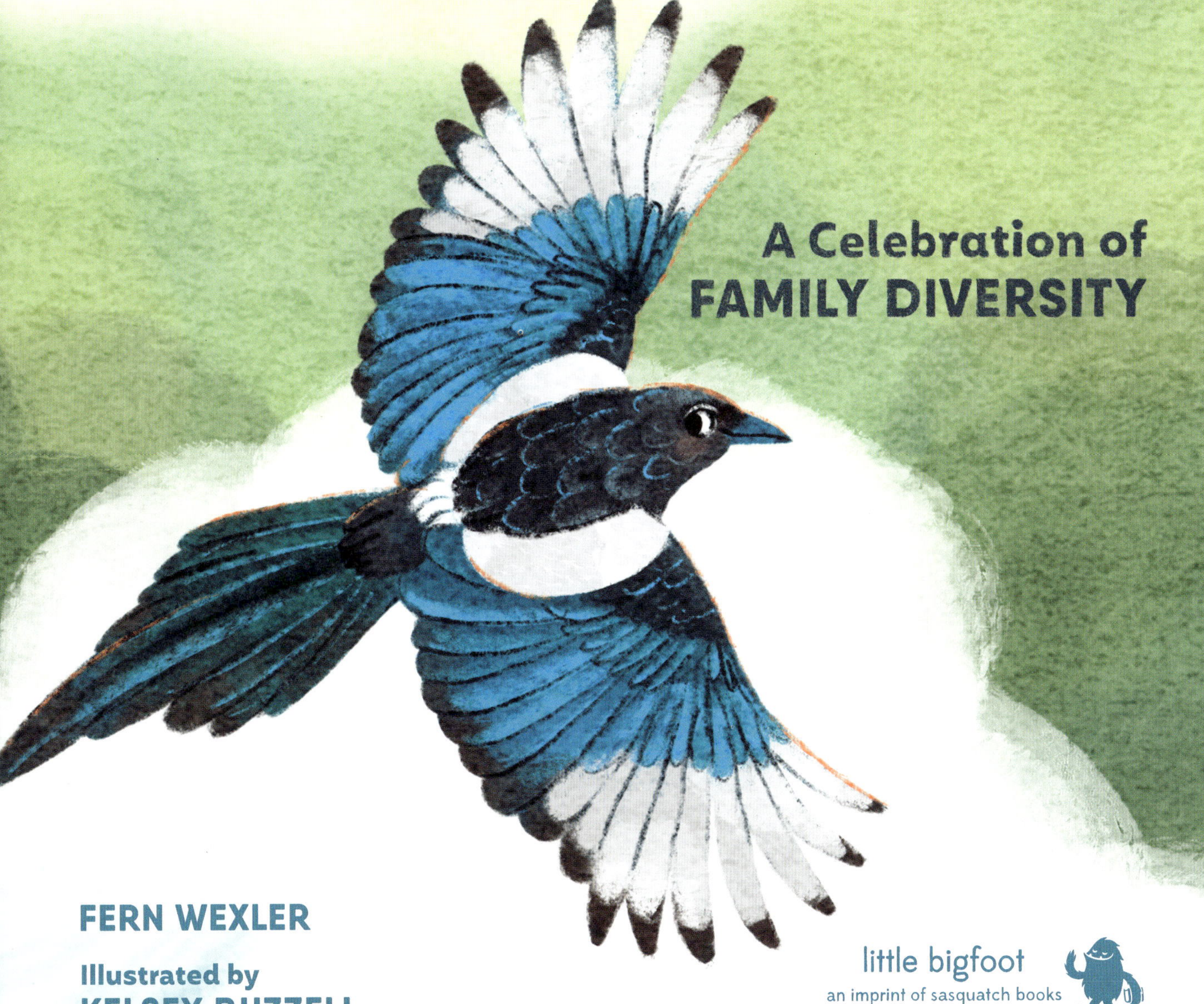

A Celebration of **FAMILY DIVERSITY**

FERN WEXLER

Illustrated by
KELSEY BUZZELL

little bigfoot
an imprint of sasquatch books
seattle, wa

Have you ever wondered what it would be like to be a bird with wings and feathers and a sharp, pointy beak?

Maybe you have noticed bird families
outside your window or in your backyard
and wondered what it would be like
to grow up in a family of birds.

Baby birds and their parents spend so much time hiding in their nest that it's difficult to see how the parents take care of the babies.

But if you look closely, you may notice that
some birds have families just like yours!

Your family may be like a Blue Jay family.

Blue Jay parents work together
to raise their babies.

Mom and dad both work hard to look after their chicks and teach them how to fly, squawk, and find their own food.

Sometimes they even teach their babies how to make the sounds of other birds!

Maybe your family is like an Emu family.

Emu dads raise their babies all by themselves.
They incubate the eggs by sitting on them
to keep them warm for eight weeks.

Once their chicks hatch, they protect them and make sure they don't get into any trouble.

No matter what happens, Emu dads can be trusted to keep their kids safe.

Your family might be like a Ruby-Throated Hummingbird family.

Ruby-Throated Hummingbird moms take care of their babies by themselves. It's hard work for such a small bird!

They bring their babies tiny bugs, like mosquitoes, to eat. They also make sure that the nest is big enough to fit their babies until they're all grown up and ready to leave.

Perhaps your family is more like a Black Swan family.

Lots of baby Black Swans grow up with two dads. Black Swan dads share everything equally and take turns keeping their eggs warm and caring for their babies after they've hatched.

When their babies get tired of swimming and looking for tasty plants to eat, their dads let them ride on their backs to rest.

You could have a family
like a Laysan Albatross.

Many Laysan Albatross babies have two moms. For several months before their babies hatch, the moms take turns sitting on the eggs to keep them warm.

After their babies break out of their shells, one mom stays with them all the time to keep them safe and dry, while the other mom hunts for food and brings them fresh squid and fish right from the ocean.

Or is your family like a Common Merganser's?

Not all Common Mergansers raise their own babies. Some moms lay eggs in another Common Merganser's nest. The nesting merganser sits on the eggs and then adopts the babies that hatch.

Sometimes a merganser will give her babies to a mom with more experience. When she gets older, she'll raise her own babies and help other moms raise theirs.

If a baby merganser gets lost, another mom will take them in and raise them with her other nestlings.

Whether a Common Merganser adopts or raises her own babies, she cares for all of them equally, teaching them how to dive for fish and fly south for the winter.

Your family may be like an Acorn Woodpecker's family.

Acorn Woodpeckers work together in groups to raise their babies. This means the babies live with really big families! They can have three moms, five dads, and seven older brothers and sisters all helping them grow up and become the best woodpeckers they can be.

When Acorn Woodpecker babies grow up, they help their parents raise the next generation, just like their older siblings helped raise them!

Not every person is born with a family.
Not every bird is either.

Australian Brush-Turkeys hatch, all on their own, out of a nest made from dead leaves and grass. They learn to be a bird without any help from a mom or dad. They even teach themselves how to fly.

When the Brush-Turkeys get a bit older, they find other turkeys their own age to live with.

They sleep together, find food together, and keep each other out of trouble.

Human and bird families help their babies by teaching them new things.

Your parents might teach you how to ride a bike.

A bird's parents might teach them where to find the best place to sing from,

or the coziest place to roost at night,

or where to find the most delicious berries.

Every person's and every bird's
family looks different,

and they show their love for
each other differently, too.

No matter what your family
looks like, remember . . .

families of a feather love together,
and everyone deserves to be loved.

MORE ABOUT THE BIRD FAMILIES

ACORN WOODPECKER: Acorn Woodpeckers are social woodpeckers that live in Oregon and California, as well as in some parts of Arizona, New Mexico, and Texas. Their range continues through Mexico and across Central America into northern Colombia. They are known for making massive acorn caches in trees, which can be filled with hundreds, if not thousands, of acorns. While not every Acorn Woodpecker participates in cooperative breeding, which is the process of many birds working together to raise their babies, most of them do. Many of the helper birds are not allowed to participate in mating if they were hatchlings the previous year; this ensures they have practice before raising babies of their own.

BLACK SWAN: Black Swans are a species of swan found in Australia and New Zealand, though they have been introduced to other parts of the world. They eat aquatic plant material and rarely venture on land to forage because their heavy bodies are designed to swim instead of walk. Approximately one-quarter of all Black Swan pairings are between two males, and they will mate with a female before chasing her away to raise the nest themselves once she has laid eggs.

AUSTRALIAN BRUSH-TURKEY: Australian Brush-Turkeys are a common urban bird in certain areas of Australia. They hatch completely precocial, which means they can walk and find food almost immediately after they hatch, and are even able to fly shortly after their feathers have dried. Their nests are large mounds which incubate the eggs inside of them, similar to how certain reptiles nest. The chicks grow up on their own but form small foraging groups after becoming juveniles.

BLUE JAY: A common bird in most of the midwestern and eastern United States and Canada, Blue Jays are loud and bossy birds with bright blue feathers and black and white markings. They can mimic the calls of other birds and use this to scare other birds away from food sources so they can take the best food for themselves. Despite their bad reputation, they are beautiful and distinct backyard birds enjoyed by many. They typically mate for life and share nest-building and parenting duties.

COMMON MERGANSER: Common Mergansers are found throughout the United States and Canada. They dive underwater to hunt fish with their pointed bills. Female Common Mergansers often adopt other babies when another female lays eggs in her nest, or if lost chicks join her because she looks like their mother, or when a younger female gives chicks to her because of her prior experience with raising them. One champion merganser mother had 76 ducklings to take care of!

LAYSAN ALBATROSS: Laysan Albatrosses can primarily be found soaring above the Pacific Ocean. They have wingspans of more than six feet long and can drink salt water to keep themselves hydrated during their long sabbaticals at sea. They have prominent nesting colonies on islands like Oahu, where more than 30 percent of the pairs are made up of two females who will mate with a neighboring male to produce an egg.

EMU: Emus are the second-largest bird in the world at more than five and a half feet tall, and are native to Australia. They cannot fly and instead have long legs that they use to travel great distances. They enjoy eating bugs and plants. Males raise their babies alone and fight fiercely to protect their young both before and after they hatch from their huge green eggs. They will often adopt stray babies who may have gotten lost.

RUBY-THROATED HUMMINGBIRD: Ruby-Throated Hummingbirds breed in most of the eastern half of the United States. They drink nectar and eat small bugs that they catch while flying. Only the male Ruby-Throated Hummingbirds have red throats. The male performs aerial courtship, and then the females do the work of raising their young alone, including all nest-building prior to laying their eggs.

LEARN MORE

The Cornell Lab of Ornithology All About Birds - AllAboutBirds.org

National Geographic Kids - kids.nationalgeographic.com/animals/birds

For Lisa, Chris, Ian, and all the other educators who inspired me to teach —FW

To Ollie and Idgie —KB

Printed in China by Dream Colour Printing Ltd. in October 2024

LITTLE BIGFOOT with colophon is a registered trademark of Blue Star Press, LLC

29 28 27 26 25 9 8 7 6 5 4 3 2 1

Editors: Michelle McCann, Christy Cox, and Avalon Radys
Production editor: Isabella Hardie
Designer: Anna Goldstein

Library of Congress Cataloging-in-Publication Data is available.

ISBN: 978-1-63217-445-1

Sasquatch Books
1325 Fourth Avenue, Suite 1025
Seattle, WA 98101

SasquatchBooks.com